Jack

Written and illustrated by

Chris Priestley

Hodder
Children's
Books

37632

a division of Hodder Headline Limited

for Sally

ACKNOWLEDGEMENTS

I would like to thank the London Metropolitan Archive, the National
Meteorological Library and Archive, the National Portrait Gallery,
the Museum of London, the Royal Society, the British Library, the Cambridge
University Library and Norfolk Libraries for their help. I am also particularly
indebted to the work of Horace Bleackley, Roy Porter, Christopher Hibbert
and Lucy Moore in the writing of this book and also to Peter Linebaugh's book
The London Hanged, as it was here that I first read of Jack Sheppard's amazing life.

The illustration on page 33 is based on Plate 9 of *Industry and Idleness*
by William Hogarth. The quotations in Chapter 9 are taken from Langley's
An Accurate Description of Newgate, London 1724.

Text and illustrations copyright 2001 © Chris Priestley
Published by Hodder Children's Books, 2001

Cover photograph courtesy of the Mary Evans Picture Library.
Cover illustration by Stuart Haygarth

The right of Chris Priestley to be identified as the author and
illustrator of this Work has been asserted by him in accordance
with the Copyright, Designs and Patents Act 1988.

ISBN 0340 788356
10 9 8 7 6 5 4 3 2 1

A catalogue record for this book is available from the British Library.

Printed by The Guernsey Press Company Ltd, Guernsey, Channel Islands.

Hodder Children's Books
a division of Hodder Headline Limited
338 Euston Road
London NW1 3BH

Contents

Map of London 4

About Time 6

1. The Metropolis 7

2. Beginnings 12

3. Shop-boy 19

4. Jack the Lad 28

5. Jonathan Wild 39

6. Jack the Jail-breaker 43

7. Fame 48

8. The Kneebone Robbery 53

9. Newgate 59

10. The Trial 66

11. On the Run 71

12. Blueskin's Sharp Penknife 77

13. The Great Escape 83

14. A Thousand Visitors 93

15. The Tyburn Way 101

16. The Hanging Tree 108

17. Revenge 114

18. The End? 119

Glossary 122

Index 128

Jack Sheppard's LONDON

HAMPSTEAD

THE TYBURN GALLOWS

TYBURN RD.   OXFORD ST.   ST. GILES   HOLB...

SOHO   LONG ACRE   DRURY LANE   WYCH ST.

TYBURN LANE

HYDE PARK   MAYFAIR   LEICESTER SQUARE   COVENT GARDEN   THE STRAND

PICCADILLY   CHARING CROSS

KNIGHTSBRIDGE   WHITEHALL   RIVER T...

WEST-MINSTER   LAMBETH

HORSE FERRY

About Time

*During the period in which Jack's
story takes place, the official and
legal start of the New Year was
25 March (Lady Day). So although
Jack's baptism record says 5 March
1701, we would call it 1702, because
our New Year starts on 1 January.
This and other similar dates have been
modernised throughout this book.*

CHAPTER 1

The Metropolis

*I*t is 1702. A little over fifty years ago, there was civil war and revolution here - Oliver Cromwell had the king's head lopped off in this very city. Less than forty years ago plague stalked the streets of London and the Great Fire roared through it.

But now it is thriving; now it is bursting at the seams. Small by twenty-first century standards, it will soon be the biggest city of the eighteenth-century world.

Thousands of merchant ships sail in and out of the Thames and the quayside warehouses are bulging with booty from all over the world: sugar from the West Indies, spices from the

East, ivory from Africa, tea from China and tobacco from America.

There are foreign visitors and tourists, and thousands of immigrants live here. With wages much higher than in the rest of the country, hordes of hopeful young people arrive each year to seek their fortune.

To the west, developers are building wide streets and grand squares bordered by fine houses. Towering over everything is Sir Christopher Wren's new (as yet unfinished) cathedral. London Bridge is still the only bridge, and the river is bustling with boats.

Londoners hurry by, dressed in expensive wigs, embroidered waistcoats and silk stockings. And that's just the men! But there is another side to all this...

The city's old heart is still a tangled knot of dark lanes and alleys. Maps of it look like a cross-section through an anthill, and it must seem that way too. The population of this small city has almost tripled over the last hundred years to 575,000 people.

The streets are jammed with traffic. Coaches, carriages and carts rumble by. Animals low and bleat as they are herded through the streets on their way to be slaughtered. Dogs, cats and rats rifle through the rubbish. Red kites squabble over discarded offal from the meat markets.

The air is polluted. Thousands of tons of sulphurous sea-coal arrive each year from Tyneside to be burnt in fireplaces and as fuel for London's blacksmiths, brick-makers, bone-boilers and brewers. Soot blackens the buildings, smoke hangs over the city. There are thick, choking fogs.

Chamber pots are tipped into overflowing basement vaults or outdoor cesspits, to be emptied by the "night-soil" man. The cobbled streets are littered with dung. London stinks.

Londoners fall victim to all kinds of diseases to which they have no cure. Surgery is performed without an anaesthetic. Lives are often cut short. Half the population is under 21.

No one trusts the water and no one drinks it. Everyone - children included - drinks beer instead. Alcohol is the drug of London's poor and many are now addicted to a dangerous new drink called Geneva, or gin.

A rich man might spend more on wine than a working man could hope to earn in a lifetime. Some spend more on a wig than many people earn in a year. The gap between rich and poor is wide and ugly.

Down at the docks, the rotting body of Captain Kidd the pirate has been creaking back and forth for a year now; hung in a metal cage as a warning to sailors who might be tempted to follow his trade.

There are public executions, but you do not have to be a pirate to end up swinging from the gallows at Tyburn. No, in this day and age, you can be hanged for stealing a length of cloth...

CHAPTER 2

Beginnings

*I*n March 1702/3 the world's first daily
newspaper - the Daily Courant - is published;
and it's quite a month. King William decides
to take advantage of the fine weather and goes for
a ride in Hampton Court Park. The horse stumbles
on a molehill and throws him off, breaking his
collarbone. He has been ill for a while and
never quite recovers from the shock. He dies a
fortnight later and Queen Anne begins her reign.
We are off to war with France (again!).

But something else of importance happens this
month, though it goes almost completely unnoticed
at the time. It is the birth of someone who will
become one of the most famous men of his day.

On 5 March Thomas Sheppard, an East End carpenter, takes his baby son to be baptised. The boy is only a day old, so his mother, Mary, is left behind at their home in Whit's Row. They live in Spitalfields, just outside the city walls of London.

They make their way to their parish church of St Dunstan's in Stepney where the baby is named John... though he will always be known as Jack. All parents are eager to baptise their children; they think the christening service will guard the baby against illness.

Because this is a dangerous time for the little fellow. Thomas and Mary already have a child buried in the graveyard - a boy, also christened John. He died the year before when he was only three years old.

There is little or no defence against disease and the death of children is horribly common,

13

especially among the poor, with maybe one in three dying before their fifth birthday.

Wealth does not necessarily make you immune - only five of Queen Anne's children are born alive (though she has been pregnant eighteen times!). Of them, just one, William, survives infancy, only to die aged eleven in 1700.

As if life is not dangerous enough, in November 1703, when Jack is only a year and a half old, a terrifying hurricane rips through London. It is called the Great Storm and it tears off roof tiles and chimney stacks, sending them crashing down into the streets.

The Thames floods its banks. Many people are killed and scores injured. The merchant fleet is all but destroyed on the river. Out to sea, twelve warships sink within sight of land with the loss of over a thousand men.

And Oliver Cromwell's head blows off! When Charles II was restored to the throne, Cromwell's 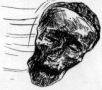 body had been dug up (he had died two years before), hanged and beheaded at Tyburn gallows

and the head stuck on a spike on top of
Westminster Hall. After twenty-five years up
on the roof, it flies off and lands in the street.

Baby Jack survives and grows and soon he
is able to explore the world around him with
his older brother Tom. So what is Spitalfields
like? What are the sights and sounds that will
greet him when he goes outside?

Surprisingly, the first language he hears
might be French. His neighbourhood is home

to thousands of Huguenots - Protestant refugees from Catholic France. In some streets it is rare to hear English spoken at all.

In the narrow lanes and alleys all around him, weavers are busy at hundreds of looms. Not just weaving, either, but dyeing and pattern drawing, cutting and stitching. The cloth they produce is worn by the wealthier folk to the west. It is silk, and the Huguenots have sewn up the business.

And French is not the only foreign language Jack might hear. There are thousands of Jewish people living in the East End, from Portugal and Spain, and, more recently, from Germany and Poland. There is a huge local Irish community.

Then there are the thousands of Africans and African Americans - servants, seamen and escaped slaves; a black face is not an unusual sight at all in eighteenth-century London. Oriental sailors from East India Company ships wander up from the docks.

Spitalfields has a lively fruit and vegetable market but Jack will also smell the fumes from the Truman brewery and see the smoke rising from the brick-works and lime-kilns of Brick Lane. This is an industrial area, grimy and polluted and home to terrible poverty.

Just as parents have to cope with the death of children, children often lose their parents while still young. When Jack is just a boy, his father dies, leaving his mother alone to look after him and Tom and his younger sister Mary. Without his income or a pension, life becomes more and more difficult for the Sheppard family.

These are hard times and poor little Mary Sheppard doesn't survive them. She dies a couple of days before Christmas 1708. Mrs Sheppard cannot cope and the family is split up. She and Tom go into service and Jack is sent to the new workhouse school in Bishopsgate Street in the City.

The children here are harshly treated and made to work long hours. They are given menial jobs to do, to prepare them for a life of graft. They are taught to read and write, but they are never taught too much, just in case they get ideas above their stations.

They are lumped in with vagabonds and beggars who have been taken off the streets. Inmates brew their own beer and eat almost nothing but bread and cheese (but then that is pretty much what all poor people eat).

The conditions are deliberately severe in the hope that this will instill discipline and obedience in the poor. Children are even more likely to die here than at home and many do not leave the workhouse alive.

Jack will have to have his wits about him if he is to survive this place.

CHAPTER 3

Shop-boy

*L*uckily for Jack, he only has to endure the workhouse for a couple of years before he escapes. The widowed Mrs Sheppard is in service to a tradesman called William Kneebone and he has offered young Jack a job and a roof over his head at his shop. Jack sets off through the busy streets of the city for the Strand.

Heavy signs creak on chains hung from wrought iron brackets. Copper or gold or painted wood, they are the neon signs of their day, each one bigger or brighter than the last as they fight for the attention of passers-by.

The streets ring with the shouts of hawkers and pedlars. There are women selling cheap snacks like oysters or pies, and men selling sermons, books, ballads and the "Last Dying Speeches" of people condemned to death.

Hackney carriages - horse-drawn taxis - roll by and sedan chairs are bundled along the pavements. Sedan chairs are a kind of cubicle on poles in which people are carried along by two strong men; they will knock you flying if you do not get out of the way.

After thirty-five years of building, St Paul's Cathedral is finished, still clean and white before the smoky London skies have worked on it. The huge lead dome is visible for miles around and there is a fantastic view from the top on a clear day.

Jack exits the city walls at Ludgate, heading west into the bustling world beyond; London has long since burst through its old boundaries. Jack crosses over the Fleet Bridge and on to Fleet Street, past Mrs Salmon's Waxworks whose weird and wonderful exhibits include *Margaret Countess of Heningbergh, Lying in on a Bed of State, with her Three hundred and*

Sixty-Five Children, all born at the one Birth!

The Strand itself is a long road running along the north bank of the River Thames between Charing Cross and Fleet Street, joining Westminster to the City. Once there had been bishops and courtiers living here in mansions, but now it is mostly lined with smaller houses and yet more shops.

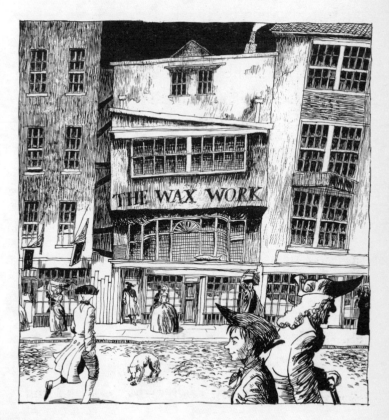

Kneebone is a woollen draper, a dealer in woollen cloth, and, as a shop-boy, Jack fetches and carries rolls of fabric as customers come and go with their orders. He gets a feel for the value of cloth; a taste for the fine clothes he will never be able (honestly) to afford.

Shopping is already one of London's major attractions. It is in these busy shops that the sweat of the Spitalfields silk-weavers is turned into gold, and the well-off can keep up with the latest fashions. And what are the latest fashions? Women's waists are slenderised by crushing whalebone corsets and their low-cut dresses are supported by huge round hoops. They use the richest fabric they can afford and decorate it with ribbons and bows, embroidery and lace. They paint their faces with poisonous lead-based make-up.

Men wear flared knee-length coats over knee-length breeches, with silk stockings and leather shoes. They carry swords and canes and wear three-cornered hats. Older men who can afford them are still wearing huge and expensive periwigs, parted in the middle and tumbling over their shoulders.

Younger men and the fashion-conscious are starting to wear smaller tie-wigs that they fasten at the back with a bow of black ribbon. Their own hair is shaved off, and the wigs are stuck to their bald heads.

As well as shops, there are lots of places to eat and drink. There are dozens of coffee houses in the area, where you can drink not only coffee, but chocolate or tea or brandy. Different sorts of people go to different coffee houses. Fops pose down at Man's at Charing Cross, and you might find

Sir Isaac Newton and Dr Edmund Halley (of Halley's Comet fame) and other bigwigs of the Royal Society down at the Grecian.

Gentlemen hold their business meetings here, smoke their pipes and read the newspapers. Runners are sent around the coffee-houses with news-flashes. So what is in the news?

Well, in the summer of 1714 the Queen dies. In September, the new king's barge looms out of the night at Greenwich and the German George Ludwig, Elector of Saxony, steps ashore as King George I. A Jacobite rebellion is crushed.

Of particular interest to our story, though, are the escapes of these Jacobites from Newgate Prison in 1715. One gets the Keeper drunk and locks up the staff before escaping using duplicate keys; another leads a break-out from the exercise yard and just runs out. A third walks out dressed as a visitor. And the Earl of Nithsdale escapes from the Tower of London dressed as a woman. Maybe Jack is reading the papers too.

On the morning of 22 April, the sky grows darker and darker and a huge shadow races towards the city. At ten past nine there is a total eclipse of the sun. Dr Halley and invited guests observe it from the roof of the Royal Society's house, just up the road in Fleet Street. The sky is clear and it becomes dark enough to see Jupiter, Mercury and Venus. An amazing sight - and an alarming one to the superstitious, who believe eclipses to be bad omens.

But what do Londoners do for entertainment in a world without TV, films or computers? A French visitor to London thought that "anything that looks like fighting is delicious to an Englishman," and he does have a point.

Cock-fighting is hugely popular, the cockerels' beaks sharpened and their feet fitted with silver spurs. Bears, bulls and badgers are set upon by dogs for sport and there are bare-knuckle boxing matches and sword fights - between women as well as men. The outcomes of all these "sports" are frantically gambled over.

You can go to see the zoo at the Tower of London or pay to gawk and laugh at the mentally ill in Bethlehem Hospital - or Bedlam as it is more commonly called. You can visit a highwayman in Newgate Prison or see him hanged at Tyburn. You can even see him dissected by "anatomisers".

There is plenty of cheap entertainment around for Jack with the freak shows, comedians and acrobats of the fairs. There is the annual Bartholomew Fair at Smithfield and another at Southwark. A May Fair is held every year and there is a huge maypole in the Strand (until Sir Isaac Newton buys it for a friend as a prop for his giant telescope).

At the end of 1715, the Thames freezes solid and everyone flocks to the Frost Fair. It is as if a small town has magically appeared in the middle of the river. There are shops selling beer and pies and printing presses making souvenir posters, all standing on the glistening white ice.

But Jack's boyhood at Kneebone's shop is coming to an end. His life is about to take a new and dangerous course.

CHAPTER 1

Jack the Lad

On 2 April 1717, at the age of fifteen, Jack is apprenticed to a carpenter with the appropriate name of Wood - Owen Wood - and moves in with him and his wife and children at their house in Wych Street, just round the corner from Kneebone's place in Covent Garden.

Ordinarily an apprentice like Jack would have to pay a fee to his "master", but Kneebone persuades Wood to take the lad on, helping him to get a building contract in Hampstead.

In the past, apprenticeship had seemed a good thing, but things have changed. Apprentices are often treated as servants, and, like servants, they are often beaten. There are even instances of masters beating their apprentices to death.

Jack is bound to Wood for seven years and in that time he is not allowed to marry or work for himself. It is an offence to break the contract. Even though Jack may learn all Wood has to offer in a couple of years, Wood owns him for the full term and can employ him however he wishes.

Jack's father, grandfather and great-grandfather were all carpenters, and he has a knack for it. He learns fast and is hard working. It is here in Owen Wood's workshop that Jack gains his knowledge of tools and materials, and his understanding of locks - skills that will serve him well in the future.

London in the 1720s is in the grip of a rising crime wave. Covent Garden is infested with pickpockets or "files", who work the crowds of dawdling shoppers and busy traders.

They steal watches, snuffboxes and handkerchiefs, the wig off your head, the sword from your belt. They "dive" into your pockets for cash. They even work the crowds at hangings!

Not that cash is not always what it seems. London is rattling with counterfeit coins and coiners are guilty of treason. Sir Isaac Newton - one of the greatest minds of his (or any other) age - was once Warden and Master of the Mint, responsible for prosecuting them.

As well as the pickpockets, there are prostitutes, footpads and burglars; there are highwaymen on the heaths and smugglers on the river. They have their own slang called "cant", which is so complex it is really another language.

The government concentrates on harsher and harsher punishments for offenders. Being "pilloried" means you are held by the head and hands in a wooden contraption while being flogged or left to the mercy of the crowd. They might pelt you with rotten fruit or dung - or shower you with stones. People occasionally die from their injuries.

Prostitutes are tied to the back of a cart and whipped through the streets. Thieves are "burned in the hand" - branded with a red-hot iron bar (though for a fee you can have it dipped in water first to lessen the effect). Both are now transported to the colonies in America as "King's Seven Years Passengers" to work on the plantations (though the plantation owners prefer African slaves).

Stealing anything over the value of a shilling can get you hanged if you do not know the "neck verse", Psalm 51. "Benefit of Clergy" is an old law designed to save clerics from the noose in the days when only they could read. You proved you could read by reading Psalm 51 from the Bible - but the illiterate soon cottoned on and learnt it by heart.

Stolen goods are often fenced in pubs and alehouses and taverns are notorious dens of thieves and prostitutes, or "molls". There are literally thousands of places to buy alcohol in London and the English are enthusiastic drinkers (a sailor's beer ration is 8 pints a day!).

Fights and brawls are common and dangerous,

with so many men armed with knives and swords and even pistols.

There is a poisonous craze for a mind-numbingly hard drink called Geneva, or gin. It is bought from dealers in gloomy cellars and from tradesmen who keep it under the counter for customers in the know. Over 2 million gallons are consumed here every year.

It is 1722 and Jack has become a regular at the Black Lion tavern round the corner. He is 19 now, 5ft 4in, but powerfully built for his size. He is cocky and witty, with a slight stutter. He is popular, especially with the molls, and now he has a girlfriend - a moll called Elizabeth Lyons, known as Edgworth Bess after her home town.

Wood is losing all control over Jack. They are working on a job at an alehouse in Islington when an argument flares up. It may even have ended in blows, though Jack always denies it. There are rows in the Wood household. They try locking the door if he stays out late, but he simply breaks in through his bedroom window, to be found tucked up in bed the next morning.

And it is worse than the Woods know. Jack's fondness for the company of thieves is having its effect, and, while working for his master at the Rummer Tavern at Charing Cross, he commits his first theft - he pockets two silver spoons.

In the spring of 1723, Bess gets caught stealing a ring and is thrown in St Giles's Roundhouse in Soho. Jack goes straight round there, forces the beadle to hand over the keys and sets her free. He is instantly a hero to the working girls of Covent Garden.

At the end of July, Wood sends Jack to work on a job at the house of a piece-broker called Bains in White Horse Yard. While he is there Jack makes off with 24 yards of fustian cloth in a roll. He tries to sell it among the young lads who live locally, but he gets no offers and hides it in his trunk back at Wych Street.

A Black Lion moll called Poll Maggot suggests that Jack go back and do the Bains place again, so in the middle of the night of 1 August he lets himself into the piece-broker's house by taking out the wooden bars to the cellar window.

Jack steals bits and pieces from around the shop and grabs £7 in cash from the till on his way out. He leaves the way he came, returning the bars so neatly that no one even notices that they have been touched. Jack trots back to Poll with the loot.

The next day he turns up as bold as brass at Bains's house to finish the shutters for the shop. When Bains and his wife discover the theft, the finger of suspicion is firmly pointed at their female lodger. After all, there is no sign of a break-in.

Unfortunately things go wrong. Jack's fellow apprentice, Thomas, has told Wood he's seen some fustian in Jack's trunk. Jack finds out and, quick as a flash, he dashes back to Wych Street, nips into the house next door, breaks through into Wood's, and "steals" his own trunk before the cloth is found.

But Wood wasn't born yesterday and he has had enough. He tells Bains that Jack has been seen with the cloth. Jack decides that attack is the best kind of defence and goes straight round to White Horse Yard.

Bains threatens to prosecute Jack for the theft but it doesn't throw Jack at all. He threatens him back, accusing him of slander.

The fustian had been a gift from his poor mother. She had bought it in Spitalfields from a weaver. He'll prove it.

Mrs Sheppard is found and she backs her son up. She even spends hours wandering round

Spitalfields with Bains, pretending to search for the non-existent weaver. There is no Benefit of Clergy on burglaries over the value of five shillings. Jack could swing for this and Mary Sheppard knows it.

Bains does not buy the story. In desperation, Jack offers to send him 19 yards of the fustian and he is placated. Victims of crimes have to prosecute the suspects themselves, and Bains may think it is more trouble than it is worth.

Just in case he changes his mind, however, Jack decides to do a runner. With a little under a year of his apprenticeship to serve, he hits the road with Bess and heads for Parson's Green, a small village to the west of London. Jack finds work with a master carpenter, but breaking his apprenticeship with Wood is a serious matter. He will have to be careful.

They are spotted. By an unlucky coincidence, Owen Wood's brother just happens to live locally and he loses no time in letting Owen know where Jack is hiding. Wood carts Jack off back to London where he is thrown into St Clement's Roundhouse for the night.

The next day Jack is taken to appear before the Chamberlain at the Guildhall to answer for breaking his contract with Wood. Luckily for Jack, the Chamberlain is away from his office, and he gets a chance to calm Wood down. They reach an agreement and Jack is on his way again.

Jack returns to London and lodges at the top end of Piccadilly, working for a carpenter doing a few repair jobs around the house. He leaves at the end of October 1723 with a bundle of loot - £7 10s in cash, five large silver spoons, four silver teaspoons, six silver forks, seven gold rings, four suits and some linen.

Jack is more thief than joiner now.

CHAPTER 5

Jonathan Wild

OK, so you have had your pocket picked, your wig snatched, your house or your shop burgled: what do you do? Calling for the police will not be an option for another hundred years, remember.

Well, if you see it happening, you can yell "Stop, thief!" at the top of your voice and hope someone grabs the culprit and calls a constable or a watchman. But you might not get a very enthusiastic response.

Constables are not professional policemen. Everyone is expected to serve time as a constable but nobody wants to do it. Those who can afford it pay others to serve for them. Watchmen are usually doddery old men paid 6d a night to wander round carrying a stick and a lantern.

If you don't know who has stolen your property or where it is, you might consider consulting a wise woman or cunning man - who will try to find it by magic! But now there is another option - you can go and see Jonathan Wild.

Jonathan Wild is a thief-taker. He is not the first or only thief-taker, but he is by far and away the most successful. In fact, he calls himself, with typical modesty, the Thief-Taker General of Great Britain and Ireland.

He runs a Lost Property Office in Old Bailey. If anyone can find your stolen sword or watch, then it is Jonathan Wild. All the best people in London come to his door, and the government has even asked his advice about dealing with this terrible crime wave.

However, the reason Wild is so good at

finding stolen goods is that he knows more than he should about the theft and the thief behind it. He controls most of the criminal activity in London. He is the godfather of organised crime and modern gangsters.

It works like this. Victims of theft are happy to pay the thief if it means getting their treasured item back. Wild finds the thief and arranges the exchange, pocketing the cash. Thieves either play by Wild's rules or he has them arrested and pockets the reward. He is happy either way.

Wild rules by intimidation. When he has enough information on one of his thieves to get them hanged he puts a cross next to their name in a special book. When they are of no further use to him he "double-crosses" them and sends them to the gallows. He has destroyed any opposition by breaking up all the rival gangs of London.

Wild is in his late thirties, only a little taller than Jack, stocky and solid. He carries a silver sword and, when he wants to show off, a silver baton, though he holds no official post. He is as sly as a fox and as hard as nails. He is fearless -

he often brings criminals in single-handedly, and has the sword, dagger and gunshot scars to prove it.

He has two henchmen: Abraham Mendez, his "Clerk of the Western Road" and Quilt Arnold, his thuggish "Clerk of the Northern Road". The titles refer to the roads they supposedly keep clear of highwaymen.

Wild and Jack have met - Wild is always on the lookout for new talent - but Jack has made it clear that he is not interested. Wild smiles and compliments him on his work, but there is no room for freelance thieves in Jonathan Wild's London. This upstart will have to be put in his place.

CHAPTER 6

Jack the Jail-breaker

*J*ack and Bess live it up for a while on the proceeds from the stuff he stole in Piccadilly and then his brother Tom turns up at the Black Lion. He has only recently been burned in the hand, but if it was meant to put him off, it has definitely not worked. Anyway, what hope of honest work is there for a branded thief?

The Sheppard brothers team up and they burgle a linen-draper called Mary Cook in Clare Market, and William Phillips' house in Drury Lane. But their spree comes to an abrupt end when Tom gets himself arrested.

Tom Sheppard is charged with the Cook robbery. He stands trial in February 1724 and to save his own neck he peaches on his accomplices, his brother Jack and Edgworth Bess.

April finds Jack keeping a low profile in the Queen's Head in King Street, Covent Garden. Someone taps him on the shoulder. It's James "Hell and Fury" Sykes, one of his drinking mates from the Black Lion.

Sykes is a chairman - a carrier of sedan chairs. It's a job that calls for strength and stamina and Sykes has plenty of both. He got his nickname from his days as a running-footman. He is one of the best known athletes of his day, running races for money, famously aggressive and competitive.

Sykes tells Jack that he's got a couple of "chubs" - suckers - just round the corner at Redgate's Tavern in Seven Dials, and they are just begging to be hammered at skittles. Stupidly, Jack agrees. Stupidly, because Sykes works for Jonathan Wild.

No sooner have they got there than the double-dealing Sykes delivers him straight into

the hands of a constable, telling him that Jack
is a suspect in the Cook robbery. The constable
marches him off to Justice Parry.

Parry orders that Jack be locked up until
the following morning, when he will question
him further. Jack is marched off to St Giles's
Roundhouse and put in a cell at the top of the
jail, two floors up.

Now this is the same roundhouse that Jack
had freed Bess from the year before, so it must be
sweet for the beadle to see him come back as a

prisoner. Not so clever now, are you, he must be thinking. But Jack is about to spoil his day again.

As soon as he gets a chance, Jack takes out an old razor he has hidden in his pocket and uses it to cut away part of the metal frame from the seat of his chair. He uses this to make a hole in the ceiling, dragging his bedding underneath to soften the noise of falling plaster.

Nine o'clock at night and Jack is working loose the tiles from inside the roof. It's still early so there are plenty of people about and a tile falls and hits one of them on the head. Not surprisingly, the man kicks up a bit of a fuss.

People crowd round, yelling and pointing and calling out that a prisoner is breaking out of the roundhouse. There is nothing to lose now, so Jack bangs a hole in the roof, sending a shower of bricks and tiles clattering down into the street.

There is total mayhem, with everyone rushing this way and that. Jack drops down into the churchyard, leaps over a low wall and saunters into the crowd who are still staring up at the roof.

Jack just smiles to himself and strolls away into the night. His jail-breaking career has just begun. But Jonathan Wild will not give up quite so easily.

CHAPTER 7

Fame

Amazingly, at ten past five in the afternoon of Monday 11 May 1724 there is another total eclipse of the sun. Again the eerie shadow drops over the city, bringing a three-and-a-half minute false night. When it is over, the birds, which had all fallen silent, spring to life again and sing as if it is dawn.

It is not a good omen for Jack. A week later, he and a friend called Benson are wandering through Leicester Square when they see a commotion going on up ahead. A gentleman is arguing with a prostitute and in the confusion Benson steals his watch.

They run for it, but, unfortunately for Jack,

he runs slap-bang into the
Sergeant of the Guard of
Leicester House. The
Prince of Wales, the
future King George II,
lives here and has an
armed guard. The
Sergeant turns him
over to the
constables and they
throw him in the

nearby St Anne's Roundhouse for the night.

The following morning Bess turns up and
tries to smuggle him in a halberd spike but is
caught in the act and locked up herself. She and
Jack are hauled up before Justice Walters, who
is informed that they are both suspects in the
robberies of Philips and Cook and sends them
to New Prison, Clerkenwell.

New Prison's Keeper Captain Geary has heard
all about the recent escape and is determined that
this rascal is not going to make a fool of him. Jack
gets his first taste of fetters; he is loaded down

with irons and locked in the strongest part of the prison, high up on the top floor.

But security is not all it might be. Jack and Bess are allowed to share a cell and any number of friends and well-wishers are allowed to visit them. Everyone wants to see another escape, and they queue up to supply Jack with the tools for the job.

On the evening of Whit Sunday, 24 May, the turnkeys check on Jack and Bess and then leave them for the night. As soon as they have stepped out of the door, Jack begins filing through the links of his fetters.

That done, he files through the iron bar of the window. Then he has to deal with the much more difficult heavy oak beam that also sits across it. He bores a tight row of small holes along its length, which weakens the beam enough for him to be able to wrench part of it out.

Jack and Bess look out of the window. They can get out now, but there is still the matter of a 25-foot drop to contend with. Jack quickly comes up with a solution. He tells Bess to strip down to her last layer of clothing - her shift - and makes a rope from her dress and petticoats and their bedding.

He ties this "rope" around Bess's waist and lowers her to the yard below. Then he ties it to the remains of the oak beam and climbs down himself. It is now Whit Monday and they have escaped from New Prison only to find themselves standing in the yard of Bridewell Prison next door.

The walls of the yard are almost as tall as the window they have just climbed out of and are topped by wrought iron spikes. They will never get over them. But the door:

maybe the huge door is a possibility.

Using the bolts and locks of the door as footholds, Jack clambers up, taking some of the bedding rope with him. Once at the top he hauls Bess up beside him and then ties some of the rope to one of the spikes so she can let herself down.

In an instant he leaps down to stand beside her in the street and they walk away together into the May morning. News of the escape spreads round London like wildfire. Jack is now truly famous.

The Kneebone Robbery

$\mathcal{J}$ack next pulls off a job in Wych Street. On the night of 16 June, an apprentice called Anthony Lamb lets Jack and his accomplice Charles Grace into his master's house. They rob the lodger Mr Barton, a master tailor, of cash, bonds, notes and clothes (Jack takes an Italian silk suit for himself).

Lamb is arrested. He is described as making a "full confession" but it seems he is made of better stuff than Tom Sheppard and does not impeach his friends. He is convicted and transported to America.

Jack starts robbing with a friend from the Black Lion called Joseph Blake, who is nicknamed Blueskin because of his "dark countenance".

He is a dangerous choice of partner - and not just because he is wild and unpredictable.

Only a year ago, Blueskin shopped his accomplices as a favour to Jonathan Wild. Wild paid him an allowance while he was in jail. He had only just been released when he first met Jack.

Jack and Blueskin decide to go in for a spot of burglary. Jack knows just the place. He knows just what is in there and what it is worth. He knows all this because it is William Kneebone's place in the Strand.

Jack spends a fortnight making brief visits to the shop, cutting through two oak bars, readying them for the night of the robbery. At midnight on 12 July they break in, stealing 108 yards of broad woollen cloth, five yards of baize, two silver spoons, a hat, a handkerchief, a wig... and a penknife.

Kneebone had been warned that this might happen, and he is furious when he discovers the theft in the small hours of the following morning. He goes straight round to see Jonathan Wild. It must have made Wild's day.

Jack and Blueskin, meanwhile, branch out into highway robbery. Armed with pistols now, they rob a couple of coaches on the Hampstead Road. They ambush a drunk. A frenzied Blueskin pistol-whips and half-drowns him in a ditch before Jack steps in to stop it.

Stealing is one thing, selling the stuff is another, so they arrange to meet a fence in a Bishopsgate Street alehouse. They walk from Jack's lock-up at Westminster horse-ferry, way across the other side of town; Blueskin carries the cloth in a pack and Jack follows behind as guard and lookout.

It says something about the times that two known criminals can travel clean across London, openly carrying their ill-gotten gains, without any problem. When they finally do meet up with the fence he offers such a low price that they only part with a small amount and have to carry the rest back!

Then, one night, back at Blueskin's mother's brandy shop in Rosemary Lane, they get talking to a man who has a lock-up just along the road. They all have too much to drink and the lads start to brag about the Kneebone robbery.

The man seems very interested. He says he might be able to shift the goods, though of course he will have to see the stuff for himself. The man is William Field, and Jack is about to make a fatal mistake.

In 1720, Wild saved Field from the gallows, seeing how useful this snake-like character might be to him. Field is a fence and professional liar and informer. He will impeach almost everyone he ever works with, thirty of whom will hang.

Jack is eager to offload their booty, so they take Field off to the lock-up. He seems suitably impressed. He'll see what he can do. But the next time Jack and Blueskin go to check on their property, they find the lock-up broken into and the cloth gone.

"Field has played rob-thief with us," says Jack. But of course it is worse than that. Field will go straight to Wild and the thief-taker will have the evidence he needs.

CHAPTER 9

Newgate

Wild makes his move. On 22 July he tracks
Edgworth Bess to a brandy shop near Temple
Bar, gets her drunk and bullies her into telling
him where Jack is. He sends the bulldog-fierce
Quilt Arnold to bring him in.

The next day Arnold bursts into Mrs Blake's
brandy shop. Jack pulls a pistol on him but
Arnold keeps coming. Jack pulls the trigger
but the gun misfires and Arnold overpowers him.

That evening Jack is back in New Prison,
in the very same cell as before. The following
morning, Friday 24 July, he is hauled up before
Justice Blackerby, who packs him off to
Newgate Prison.

In the heat of the summer of 1724, Jack enters Newgate for the first time. The outside has had a £10,000 facelift after being caught in the Great Fire, but little has changed inside Newgate for the last three hundred years.

Female statues have been added to the 60-foot-high gate, and down at the feet of one of them, "Liberty", is a cat, a reference to Dick Whittington. The fifteenth-century Lord Mayor of London left money for building work on the prison and the cant for Newgate is "the Whit".

The prison is on several floors; a warren of different rooms or "wards" built into the gatehouse and into buildings on either side of it. There are debtors and felons here, male and female; a felon being someone who, like Jack, is accused of a crime that carries a death sentence.

Newgate is not really a prison in our sense of the word. The inmates here are not serving prison sentences as such - they were almost unknown at this time. Most are either, like Jack, waiting for their trial, or, having been found guilty, are waiting to receive their punishment.

Jack is taken to a room called the Lodge
and fettered. Each prisoner who enters Newgate
must pay a fee, or "garnish-money", to the
guards who are called "turnkeys". Prisoners
even have to pay a fee when they leave.

The harshness of the conditions varies depending on how much money you can afford to spend. Bedding, candles, food and drink all have to be paid for. Those with no money are thrown into the Stone Hold, a stinking cellar with no daylight where prisoners sleep on the cold stone floor.

On the Master's Side, those who have the "rhino" (ready cash) get to sleep in a bed (which they rent by the week) and warm themselves by a fire in winter (providing they pay for the coal). If they are lucky, they will get a ward away from the communal toilet which has a tendency to "annoy the air".

But the best rooms in the prison are next to the Press Yard. Anyone with the £20-£500 deposit and the 11s 6d a week rent money - which is expensive even for an apartment in the better parts of the city - can have a large and spacious room free from "ill smells". They can even have their families to stay.

On the Common Side are wards like Debtor's Hall, described as having "very good air and light." Unfortunately the "good air" comes from the fact that there is no glass in the window, which lets in "all kinds of rain, snow, sleet etc".

They might need good air too, because next to this ward is Jack Ketch's Kitchen where the hangman "boils the quarters of such men as have been executed for treason etc" before tarring them and putting them on display.

Jack is heading for the Common Side, "a most terrible wicked and dreadful place". Most men go to the Middle Ward, which is dark and dank, with no fire or beds. The Women Felon's Ward is up at the top of the building, a huge room with only one tiny window.

Dogs and chickens wander about... so do rats. Cockroaches and lice crackle underfoot. And with lice comes typhus, which is called "jail fever" here. There are regular outbreaks and it is so dangerous that doctors won't even set foot in the building. About thirty people die here every year from disease or neglect.

Passers-by hold their noses against the stench, and hurry too if they have any sense, because prisoners urinate from upstairs windows and empty their chamber pots on to the street below.

There is constant uproar. The Keeper rakes in cash from rents and the sale of ale, stout and tobacco. Visitors and inmates gamble openly and gin is brewed and sold here and given names like "Kill-Grief" and "Comfort".

Everybody is on the make. Even the prison chaplain, the Ordinary of Newgate, gets his cut. His perk is to publish and sell his Account, a short life-story of the condemned based on his efforts to get them to confess their sins. He would certainly be aware that a star like Jack is in the prison.

But Reverend Purney is ill and recuperating in the country, leaving the prisoner's souls in the care of his deputy, Reverend Wagstaff. Purney must be kicking himself. If Jack is found guilty and sentenced to hang, the Ordinary stands to make a tidy sum. His wages are £50 pounds a year, but he makes double that from the sale of his Accounts. The more famous the criminal, the better they sell.

But no one could possibly have guessed just *how* famous Jack was about to become.

CHAPTER 10

The Trial

*E*ight times a year, cases are tried at the Sessions held at the Old Bailey, on the south side of Newgate. Jack's trial is on the second day of the Sessions, Thursday, 13 August 1724.

The Old Bailey is set back from the busy street. A narrow alley leads to the Sessions House Yard where witnesses and prosecutors, jurors and spectators gather before the trial.

The judges and jury sit in the shelter of a recess under the Sessions House, but everyone else stands in the open. No one wants to be shut in with jail-fever if they can help it.

Prisoners wait in the bail dock behind a low spiked wall before being led into the court dock to stand trial. Ten years earlier, a vicious turnkey called Spurling was actually shot by one of the prisoners in full view of the judges, and in 1716 a just-convicted highwayman vaulted the wall and ran off. The prisoners are now fettered.

Jack is put in the dock and charged with the robbery of William Phillips and Mary Cook in February and of William Kneebone in July. One of the court attorneys gets to his feet.

"May it please your lordship," he says, "I am counsel for the King against the prisoner at the Bar." There is no counsel for the defence.

There is not enough evidence to convict on the first two charges, and, although he is certainly guilty, Jack is acquitted. The Kneebone robbery is a different matter altogether, however, thanks to Field and Wild.

Kneebone, the prosecutor, gives his evidence:

"The prisoner hath sometime since been my servant," he says and goes on to describe how he found his shop burgled, how he was sure it was Jack and how he went to Wild about it.

Then Jonathan Wild steps up and tells them

how Kneebone came to him for help.

"He suspected the prisoner was concerned in the fact because he had committed several rogueries thereabouts and he desired me to inquire after the goods," he says. Wild describes how he then contacted Field to help with catching Jack and getting the cloth back. But it will not be enough simply to connect Jack with the stolen goods. They will have to connect him with the robbery itself.

The prosecution calls William Field.

"The prisoner told me and Blueskin that he knew of a ken worth milling," says F A "ken" is cant for a house and "milling robbing. Field says Jack took him and Blueskin there and that Jack robbed the place while they stood as lookout. Field the fence is claiming to be a witness to the break-in.

After a few more witnesses have been called, Jack is asked what he has to say in his own defence. Jack makes no attempt to deny his guilt. Incensed by Field's testimony, he stutters out a long attack on Field, denying his claim to have been at the robbery and saying that Field knew the details of the crime only because he and Blueskin had told him.

It is not a speech designed to get Jack acquitted and the jury does not take long to return a guilty verdict. Jack is taken back to Newgate, and the following morning of Friday, 14 August, he and the other convicts are led back to the Justice Hall for sentencing.

Nine of them are sentenced to be burned in the hand and thirty-one to transportation. Six

are sentenced to death: Joseph Ward and
Robert Colthorp for highway robbery; Anthony
Upton for burglary; Stephen Fowler for shop-
lifting; Frances Sands for theft; and young
Jack Sheppard.

CHAPTER 11

On the Run

William Pitt, the Keeper of Newgate, is away, so his deputy, Bodenham Rouse, is in command of the turnkeys. There is a lot of pressure on them - no one wants a repeat of the embarrassment of the Jacobite escapes. But Jack is due to hang in a couple of weeks. What can possibly go wrong?

On the morning of Saturday, 29 August, Jack bids farewell to Lumley Davis, who has been in the Condemned Hold with him. Davis is off to be hanged at Tyburn after his own failed escape attempt. The turnkeys had neglected to relieve him of his tools, however, and he passes them on to Jack.

Jack sets to work immediately on one of the massive iron spikes on top of the doorway between the Hold and the Lodge. On Monday, Bess and Poll Maggot turn up, chatting to him through the hatch; shielding him from view, while he files away at the spike and works it loose. Amazingly, the turnkeys are drinking at a table in the same room, although a projecting wall obscures their view.

Helped by Bess and Poll, Jack squeezes through the gap, covers his leg irons under a woman's cloak, hobbles out of Newgate and into the street, where a hackney carriage is waiting.

The turnkeys cannot believe it. The newspapers marvel at it. Everyone is talking about it. Jack Sheppard has cheated the hangman after all!

Jack teams up with an old friend, the son of a Clare Market butcher, called William Page. He buys Jack a blue smock and woollen apron to disguise him as a butcher's apprentice and they scoot out of London to stay with relatives of Page's in Chipping Warden in Northamptonshire.

The appointed day of Jack's hanging comes and goes while he and Page lie low on the farm in Chipping Warden. But, for all his skill in escaping from handcuffs and prisons, Jack seems unable to escape from London.

On 8 September, with Wild and his men tearing the place apart searching for him, Jack and Page return to the City. They are recognised straight away - by a cobbler in Islington and a milkman in Bishopsgate - who, eager for a reward, raise the alarm.

Jack walks past the Old Bailey and Newgate and on down Fleet Street. He sees a tray of watches in a shop window opposite St Bride's

Church. He jams the door shut to stop anyone following him, smashes the windowpane and makes off with the goods.

But, as foolhardy as he is, Jack soon realises that Wild is watching all his usual haunts. He has got to find somewhere else to stay. Wild has an idea that Jack is heading for Stourbridge Fair and sends someone after him.

But Wild is completely wrong. Jack decides to hide out on Finchley Common, a notorious haunt of highwaymen. Despite the danger, his mate Page goes with him.

Back at Newgate, Deputy Keeper Bodenham Rouse is determined to make amends for the escape. He has posted a reward for Jack's recapture. The turnkeys who let Jack get out are drafted into a posse and on 10 September, acting on a tip-off, they ride out for the Common.

Jack and Page are spotted almost immediately. Jack tells Page to run, but he is not quick enough and is grabbed. Jack, of course, is a little harder to catch. He manages to get away, finds an old stable and hides away in the hayloft.

Buried in the hay, Jack hears the rumble of approaching horses. The posse arrives and they search the farm. Jack holds his breath. They don't see him. They walk right by him. Maybe he'll get away after all.

Suddenly, the farmer's daughter spots Jack's foot sticking out of the hay and shouts out. With the game up, Jack leaps down, ready to fight his way out - only to find himself looking down the barrels of four cocked pistols.

Jack gives in. He is handcuffed and frisked. They find a couple of the watches he stole in Fleet Street and a knife hidden in his pocket. That same afternoon, only days after his escape, poor Jack is back in Newgate.

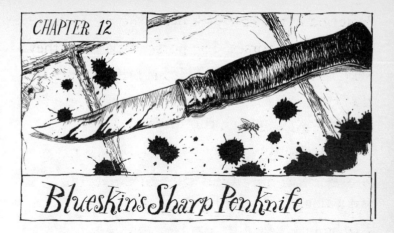

CHAPTER 12

Blueskin's Sharp Penknife

People queue up to see the famous Jack Sheppard, happy to pay the three shillings and six pence entrance fee they charge. On Sunday when he is brought up to the chapel in chains and irons, the place is packed.

By law, Jack's execution can't take place until after the next Old Bailey Sessions in October. Almost immediately, tools - files, a chisel, and a hammer - are found hidden in his cell. Jack is moved to the "Castle", up on the third floor of the gate, considered to be the strongest ward in Newgate.

Dimly lit by a heavily barred window, Jack is chained by the ankles to a massive padlock

fixed to a huge metal staple in the floor of
the cell.

Not that it seems to make much difference
to Jack. On 7 October the turnkeys find him
wandering round the room, having picked the
padlock with the help of a nail. They fetch
heavier irons, a bigger padlock and put a
pair of handcuffs on him.

The heavyweight boxing champion, James
Figgs comes to see him. The fighter promises
to have a drink with Jack when he passes by
on his way to Tyburn. Kneebone visits and is
upset to see the effect that the irons are having
on Jack's wrists and ankles. Even Bains and
Wood make the trip.

Wild was furious that he had been beaten
to Jack's arrest so he now moves on Blueskin
Blake. In October, Wild, Abraham Mendez
and Quilt Arnold turn up at Blueskin's lodgings.
Arnold bangs on the door and demands that he
open it. Blueskin refuses. Arnold kicks it in.

Blueskin pulls a knife on them, threatening
to kill the first man who walks in the room.

But he's out of his league.

"If you don't deliver your penknife immediately," says Arnold stepping forward, "I'll chop your hands off." Blueskin drops the knife and they take him in.

On the way to the Justice of the Peace, Blueskin tells Wild of his fear of being "anatomised" by surgeons. Bodies of the hanged "belong" to the hangman and have to be bought back or they are sold to surgeons for dissection. Wild grins and promises him a decent burial.

At Blueskin's trial on the 14th, Field, Arnold, and Mendez all queue up to give evidence against him. Slippery William Field, who Jack and Blueskin swear had not even been present at the robbery, testifies again.

Now Field subtly changes his story of the Kneebone burglary. At Sheppard's trial, Field made out that Blueskin was merely Jack's accomplice, but now he claims that Blueskin also entered the house and robbed alongside him. Having dealt with Jack, Wild is putting a noose around Blueskin's neck.

Maybe Blueskin has been working with Wild and Field all along, helping them to trap Jack. If so, then he has been double-crossed. In desperation he pleads with Wild in the bail dock. Maybe Wild could try to get his sentence reduced to transportation?

"You may as well put in a good word for me as for another person," says Blueskin. But Wild has no further use for Blueskin.

"You are most certainly a dead man," he says coldly, "and shall be tucked up very speedily."

All hope gone, Blueskin goes berserk. In a flash he produces a penknife and slashes at the thief-taker's throat. Wild collapses, blood gushing from the wound and is taken away.

When questioned later, Blueskin swears it was an unpremeditated attack. If he had planned it, he says, he would have made sure he had "a better knife, which would have cut his head off directly." Then he would have tossed the head into the Sessions Yard rabble.

A ballad is sung shortly after Blueskin's attack on Wild. It is called Newgate's Garland;

> *Ye fellows of Newgate, whose fingers are nice*
> > *At diving in pockets, or cogging of dice;*
> *Ye sharpers so rich, who can buy off the noose;*
> *Ye honest poor rogues, who die in your shoes;*
> > *Attend, and draw near,*
> > *Good news you shall hear,*
> *How Jonathan's throat was cut from ear to ear;*
> > *For Blueskin's sharp penknife hath set you at ease,*
> > *And ev'ry man round me, may rob, if he please.*

But Jonathan Wild is not dead. Luckily for him, he was wearing a thick cravat round his neck, and a group of the very surgeons so feared by Blueskin are in court. They stitch up the wound - which must have been an interesting experience: there are no anaesthetics, remember. Wild is badly injured and lucky to live.

Blueskin, of course, is condemned to death.

CHAPTER 13

The Great Escape

*N*ewgate is buzzing with the news of Blueskin's attempt on Wild's life. In the afternoon of Thursday 15 October, Jack has some special visitors. They are officials from other jails, come to have a last look at the famous prison-breaker. Captain Geary of New Prison is one of them.

Jack slyly pleads with the turnkey to come back and see him later that evening, but the turnkey tells him he is far too busy and won't be back until morning, just as Jack hoped. The turnkey suspects nothing. Jack would hardly ask for him if he was planning anything, now would he?

THE VISITORS STAY FOR AN HOUR OR SO. THEY SHARE A JOKE. THEY INSPECT JACK'S LEG IRONS AND HANDCUFFS. THEN, AT ABOUT 3 O'CLOCK IN THE AFTERNOON, THEY LEAVE. THE DOOR IS LOCKED AND BOLTED AND JACK IS LEFT ALONE

SLAM CLICK CLUNK

BUT JACK HAS FOUND A *NAIL!*

IN THE GLOOM OF THE **CASTLE** JACK USES THE NAIL TO PICK THE LOCK OF HIS **HANDCUFFS**...

CLICK

NNGH!

THEN, USING ALL HIS STRENGTH, HE **TWISTS** AND PULLS ON THE **CHAINS** THAT HOLD HIS LEGS TO THE **STAPLE** IN THE FLOOR

KECHANG

AND **BREAKS** THEM!

HE STILL HAS HIS **LEG IRONS** ON, BUT NOW HE CAN **MOVE** AROUND. HE **WRAPS** THE CHAINS ROUND HIS KNEES SO THEY DO NOT **DRAG**

SO BACK THROUGH THE **CHAPEL** AND INTO THE **RED ROOM**

THEN INTO THE **CASTLE** TO RETRIEVE HIS BLANKET...

BACK ON THE ROOF HE USES THE CHAPEL **SPIKE** TO SECURE THE BLANKET.

AND LOWERS HIMSELF DOWN ONTO A NEIGHBOURING ROOF

The turnkey who wanders into Jack's cell on Friday morning cannot believe his eyes. He raises the alarm, but of course it is all too late. When news gets out, people queue to pay the entrance fee to Newgate just to see Jack's escape route. A reward of 20 guineas is offered for his arrest.

Jack, meanwhile, is hiding out in a cowshed off Tottenham Court Road, while it pours with rain all around him. He manages to con someone into knocking his fetters off and returns to the city disguised as a beggar, to hear the buzz about his escape.

On Tuesday, 20 October he hires a room in Newport Market and sends for two molls called Kate Cook and Kate Keys. On the night of the 29th Jack breaks into the Rawlins brothers' pawnshop in Drury Lane.

The next day Jack is dressed in a fine new black suit, a tie-wig on his head, a silver sword on his hip. There is a gold watch in his pocket and a diamond ring sparkles on his finger. He hires a coach and tours the city, past his old home in Spitalfields, past the workhouse in Bishopsgate

and even under the arch of Newgate itself.

But Jack seems to have run out of ideas. His mother begs him to leave the country before he gets caught, but although he says he will, he does nothing about it. Instead he goes on a drinking binge accompanied by Moll Frisky.

Inevitably he is recognised and a constable is sent for. After performing one of the most amazing escapes in history, the drunken Jack Sheppard is caught with pathetic ease. He is

bundled into a hackney-carriage and taken back
to Newgate.

Jack is taken to the Middle Stone Room,
next to the Castle, above the arch of Newgate.
He is loaded with 300lb of fetters, handcuffs
and chains, and guarded day and night.

CHAPTER 14

A Thousand Visitors

*J*ack is the biggest show in town. The turnkeys
are raking the money in from people rushing
to Newgate to see the famous Jack Sheppard.
Over a thousand visit in the first week after his
return. They give Jack money to help ease his
stay in the prison.

There are gentlemen from the highest ranks in
society here, eager to chat for a few minutes with
the jail-breaker and have a story to tell in their
club. As for Jack, he seems to enjoy being a
celebrity, laughing and joking with all his visitors.

A journalist, Daniel Defoe, comes to see him.
Defoe tells Jack that he and his publisher, John
Applebee, will give him a chance to tell his own

story, to put his own side across. Defoe will help him write it. And they'll make sure Jack gets a decent burial.

The government is not amused that a common thief and idle apprentice is being treated like a hero for escaping from justice. On 6 November the Secretary of State, the Duke of Newcastle, writes to the Attorney-General:

> *Sir,*
>
> *His Majesty being informed of the extraordinary escapes that John Sheppard, a felon convict, has twice made out of Newgate and how very dangerous a person he is, has commanded me to signify to you his pleasure that you do forthwith cause him, in the proper course of Law, to be brought before the Court of King's Bench to the end that execution may without delay be awarded against him...*

By "dangerous" Newcastle means dangerous to them - to the government, to the establishment. Jack is threatening their authority by making them look stupid. There must not be any mistakes this time. This cocky little East End robber will have to be squashed...

So, instead of being taken to the Old Bailey next door, Jack is driven across town to Westminster, to the Court of King's Bench, in the back of a coach. Small crowds line the route, shouting and trying to catch a glimpse of him.

Jack's chains are removed as he enters the court and he is brought before the judges - including the Attorney-General, Sir Philip Yorke. It is Tuesday, 10 November 1724.

This is not a trial. The only witnesses that are required are officers from Newgate, who are there simply to confirm that this Jack Sheppard is the same man to have received the death sentence at the Old Bailey. This they do.

Jack asks that a petition for clemency he has sent to the King be read out in Court and Sir Philip agrees. Jack is then asked why it is that, if he expects clemency, he carried on his life of crime after his escape from jail. Jack blames his youth and says he was unable to work honestly. He says he had been planning to leave the country when he was taken in Drury Lane.

The judges listen stony-faced. There might be a way Jack could receive clemency, they say: he could name his accomplices. Jack replies that he has already named them - even though he has in fact only named the ones already charged or convicted. As for his escapes...

"I had not the least assistance from any person in my escapes - but God Almighty!"

This piece of blasphemy outrages the Court. Justice Powys, almost eighty years old and President of the Court, is furious. But, cocky as ever, Jack says that he'll prove he had no accomplices. If they care to replace his handcuffs, he'll give the Court an exhibition of his art, by taking them off before their very eyes.

This is the last straw. Justice Powys delivers the judgement of the Court. He directs a tirade against Jack, exaggerating his crimes out of all proportion. The death sentence is pronounced once more.

Jack does not go straight back to Newgate though. Amazingly, the Lord Chancellor of England asks to see him in private. Lord Macclesfield is curious to meet this celebrity thief - and they may have had more in common than first appears. The Privy Council is about to investigate Macclesfield for embezzlement. In 1725 Macclesfield will be found guilty of bribery and of misappropriating the huge sum of £100,000. But there is no danger of the gallows for him. He is merely fined £30,000

which he pays off
in a matter of weeks.

A huge crowd has
gathered outside
Westminster Hall, shoving and
pushing and fighting to get the best
view. Several people are hurt in the crush
and a constable trying to control the crowd has
his leg broken.

The authorities are taking no chances. The
coach carrying Jack and his jailers is heavily
guarded and forces its way through the crowd
back to Newgate.

They put Jack in the Middle Stone Room
for the night, but the next day he is back in
the Condemned Hold. There is only one other
occupant - Louis Houssart, a French barber
convicted of murdering his wife.

There had been three others, though,
earlier that morning, but they have been carted
off to the Hanging Tree. One of them was
Blueskin Blake, who went to the gallows
drunk and weeping.

The jailers at Newgate belatedly try to get their act together. Jack is guarded around the clock, weighed down with manacles and irons and chained to a staple.

On the Friday before Jack's execution, Sir James Thornhill pays him a visit. He is Sergeant-Painter to George I, a Member of Parliament and one of the most distinguished artists of the day.

There in the gloom of the Condemned Hold he sketches Jack Sheppard leaning on a table, handcuffs on his wrists. Jack is still wearing the expensive suit he stole from Rawlins' pawnshop, and around his neck is a scarf, knotted at the throat. Thornhill's study is made into an engraving and copies of it are sold in print shops around the town for years.

On Sunday, 15 November Jack enters the chapel to hear the "Condemned Sermon". The place is packed, of course, but Jack is disappointingly well behaved. That night, at midnight, the sexton from St Sepulchre's Church stands beneath the archway of Newgate, clangs his bell and begins to chant:

CHAPTER 15

The Tyburn Way

At about ten o'clock on Monday, 16 November Jack is formally handed over into the custody of Watson the Under-Sheriff in the Press Yard at Newgate, and a journeyman-smith knocks his leg irons off with a block and hammer.

Jack seems calm at first. He waits patiently while the smith sets about the fetters, but he starts to look a little worried when they do not seem to be removing his handcuffs. It is normal for the condemned to have their arms tied to their sides with heavy rope and Jack tells them so.

Watson wags his finger at him and smiles.

"You are an imp of mischief and it would be

impossible to deliver you safely to Tyburn unless you have irons on your wrists."

Jack goes crazy. He demands that the handcuffs be removed. Watson gets suspicious and gets the guards to hold him still while he frisks him. Jack struggles. Suddenly Watson lets out a yell and pulls back, blood leaking out of a gashed finger.

Hidden away in the lining of Jack's waistcoat is a clasp knife, its blade sticking out. This is Jack's last plan of escape. Recovering his good humour, he tells them how he was going to cut the rope and leap out of the cart on the way to Tyburn.

Having seen to his bleeding hand, Watson starts the ritual off once more. Jack is led out of the Press Yard, past the Condemned Hold and into the Lodge. Outside is the City Marshal holding a silver mace, waiting on horseback to lead them off with a group of his men. Watson mounts his horse and gathers his constables behind.

Behind them is a two-wheeled, open-ended cart - the tumbril. It is driven by Jack Ketch - once the name of a real and hated hangman but now the nickname for all hangmen. Accompanied by the Reverend Wagstaff, Jack is put in the cart, with the noose slung across his chest.

Finally there is the clatter of javelin men - an armed guard of turnkeys from the Wood Street Compter debtors' prison - and then a group of constables on horseback, mustering themselves to march at the rear. When everyone is in their place the City Marshal leads them away on the start of their two-mile procession.

They have hardly begun before they stop again. They draw up alongside the porch of St Sepulchre's Church and some people manage to get to the cart and shake Jack by the hand. The bell tolls away in the tower, and the sexton who kept Jack awake the night before stands on the church steps ringing a hand-bell:

"All good people pray heartily unto God for this poor sinner who is now going to his death and for whom the great bell doth toll. You who are condemned to die, repent with lamentable tears...".

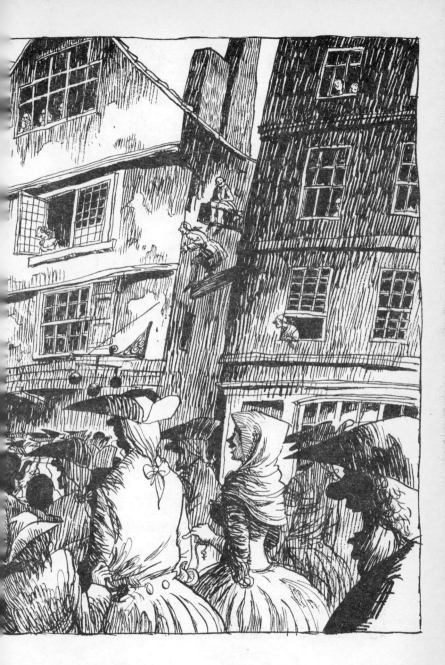

Girls gather on the steps of St Sepulchre's where the procession comes to a halt. These sobbing fans turn out whenever a handsome highwayman or daring robber is on the Tyburn Way. They throw little bunches of flowers - nosegays - into the cart; they might even steal a kiss. They do their best to lift Jack's spirits.

On now, down Snow Hill, over the Fleet river and up Holborn Hill where the road widens and the crowd fills the streets. They ride on, slower now with all the people pushing in on them, towards the Church of St Giles-in-the-Fields where people sit on the wall of the churchyard and lean out of windows.

A man darts out, squeezes through the guards and whispers something that only Jack hears, and Jack lifts his head and laughs out loud. What could he find so amusing at a time like this? Meanwhile, old Wagstaff drones on in his ear, reciting the prayer for the dead and endlessly asking him questions. It seems like an age before they pull up alongside the house of James Figg on the Oxford Road.

Jack is delighted to see that, just as he had promised, the grinning boxer is standing in the doorway with a pint of sack. Jack is freezing in his thin suit and the warmth of the drink and Figg's gesture must be welcome now that the dreaded gallows is looming into sight.

CHAPTER 16

The Hanging Tree

*T*he Tyburn gallows is a weird sight. It is triangular, with three legs and three crossbeams, giving it three framed sides - one of its names is the Sheriff's Picture Frame. Others are the Tyburn Tree, or Triple Tree, or the Deadly Never-Green. It is designed so that groups can be hanged at one time.

The crowd is enormous. Some say there are as many as 200,000 people here. Hanging days are called Hanging Fairs or Hanging Matches and apprentices are given the day off to see them, in the hope they might be frightened into respectable behaviour. But Jack is a hero to them now.

The spectators have been standing here for

hours on this cold November morning, making sure they get the best view they can. Some have even paid for seats in Mother Proctor's Pews, a grandstand built by the widow Proctor every hanging day. A large hearse stands nearby, eyed suspiciously by the crowd who are always on the lookout for the hated surgeons.

The City Marshal clears the area around the gallows and rings it with guards. Then, with a flick of the reins, the hangman brings the cart trundling into the arena and into the grim shadow of the gallows.

Jack is given the chance to "whittle" - to impeach his accomplices. Under-Sheriff Watson rides over and begins to question him about his crimes. Jack stammers out answers, confessing to his guilt in the Cook and Phillips burglaries despite his acquittal. He is on surprisingly good form, once again angrily accusing Field of lying.

Jack is holding a pamphlet entitled A Narrative of All the Robberies, Escapes, etc, of Jack Sheppard. It has been advertised in the papers. He hands it to someone, shouting that it is to be published forthwith as his last dying confession. This stunt is probably Daniel Defoe's idea: the Narrative sells like hot cakes and publisher Applebee rakes in the cash.

Watson's questions are all answered. The last prayer is said. The rope is tied to the crossbeam and the noose is slipped over Jack's head and around his neck. Jack's eyes are covered. Watson bows to the hangman, who jumps from the cart, grabs the horse by the bridle and leads him off.

The cart disappears from under Jack's feet and he is left swinging in the air. The rough hemp rope bites into his throat. The crowd moans as he jerks and kicks out against the pain; kicks out against the theft of his life. "Dancing in the Sheriff's Picture Frame," it is called.

There is no
romance here.
However brave the
condemned, this is a cruel
and ugly death. Fingers twist
and eyes bulge out from their
sockets. Bowels and bladders empty
- there is nothing in being hanged but
a "wry neck and a wet pair of breeches," it was
said with grim gallows humour.

The heavier you are, the faster you die,
as your body weight pulls against the noose.
Sometimes friends or family manage to grab
the legs of the hanged and add their weight to
speed the process. Jack is small and he is slowly
and painfully choking to death.

He dangles there for about fifteen minutes
until a soldier suddenly leaps out of the crowd,
bursts through the cordon and climbs the
gallows. Dozens follow and they take Jack's
body from him as he cuts it down. Whether out
of sympathy or the fear of a riot, Watson and
the City Marshal do nothing to stop them.

Suddenly the hearse begins to edge forward; the crowd goes berserk, believing surgeons are about to snatch the body. They launch an attack, chase the driver off with a volley of stones and set the horses loose. They smash the coach to pieces.

But the hearse belongs to a different kind of vulture: it has been hired by Applebee for another publicity stunt. The plan had been to race in and grab the body and give it the burial Defoe had promised in St Sepulchre's Churchyard. It has backfired.

Jack may still be alive - some later say they saw signs of life - and there are friends who want to try to resuscitate him. But the crowd is hysterical now, obsessed with the threat of anatomisers. They grab and maul at the body and carry it this way and that for ten minutes or more until all hope of life is gone.

In the end, the battered body is pulled out of the scrum and taken to Covent Garden, to the Barley Mow tavern in Long Acre, but a rumour soon spreads that it has been stolen. The hysteria about surgeons erupts again and a riot breaks out.

Guards are sent for and they march on the mob with fixed bayonets. The crowd sensibly disperses but the ringleaders are arrested.

Jack's body is finally delivered into the hands of a "gentleman" who has promised to ensure his safe burial. Who is it? Could it be that Defoe has managed to make up for the earlier fiasco? We don't know.

That night, the coffin is carried down Long Acre under armed guard through a huge crowd but there is no further violence; all is calm now. A hush descends and the service is spoken. A little before midnight on 16 November 1724, at the age of twenty-one years and eight months, Jack Sheppard is slowly lowered into his grave outside St Martin-in-the-Fields.

But that is not quite the end of the story.

CHAPTER 17

Revenge

*L*ondon has turned against Jonathan Wild. Everyone was enjoying the exploits of young Jack Sheppard and now Wild has spoiled their fun. No one had liked Wild, but they thought he was a necessary evil. Now they are after his blood.

Wild stupidly gets involved in a pointless feud with a pub landlord called Edwards, who has one of Wild's men arrested. Wild and Quilt Arnold attack the constables and free him. Wild ends up looking like the gangster he really is, and he decides to lie low for a while.

But on 15 February 1725, Wild is arrested at his office in Old Bailey, along with Quilt Arnold. The two men are taken to the magistrate and Wild is charged with aiding the escape of a "highwayman" (though the man is actually working as a smuggler). Then he is taken to Newgate.

Like a Mafia boss, Wild carries on running the organisation from prison, using his cell as his office. As we have already seen, an inmate's experience of Newgate varies according to the wealth of the prisoner. Wild has the best that money can buy.

But the tide is turning. Newspapers are starting to attack Wild. A warrant is issued charging him with running a "Corporation of Thieves". Wild publishes a list of the sixty-five people he helped to hang - but this only makes him look worse.

On 15 May, the Thief-Taker General stands in the dock of the Old Bailey to hear the jury return a guilty verdict. He has been far too clever to be convicted of theft, and in the end the only thing they can make stick is a charge of receiving stolen goods - while he was in Newgate!

So the most powerful criminal Britain has so far produced gets done for handling some stolen lace. A pathetic crime, but still a capital offence. The same judge who sentenced Jack to death the year before now sends Wild to the Triple Tree.

Knowing the reception he is likely to get from the London crowd, Wild takes a drug overdose, but he vomits before it kills him. He is still woozy the next morning when he is put on Jack Ketch's cart, dressed in his nightgown and wig.

The route to Tyburn is lined with even more people than had turned out for Jack's send-off. But instead of cheers and nosegays, Wild is jeered and pelted with stones, mud and dung. One stone cuts his head open and blood trickles down his face.

Three others are hanged before him, but it is Wild the crowd have come to see. They threaten to attack the hangman if he does not get on with it. The noose is pulled around Wild's throat, rubbing against the scar from Blueskin's penknife.

As the cart moves from under his feet, Wild desperately grabs one of the corpses hanging next to him, but the hangman prises him free and Wild is finally "turned off".

Wild is buried in secret, but the secret is not kept. A few days later the grave is robbed and on 15 June 1725, the Daily Journal reports that:

Last Sunday morning there was found upon

Whitehall Shore, in St Margaret's Parish, the

skin, flesh, and entrails (without any bones)

of a human body... the surgeon who attended,

gave it his opinion that it could be no other

than the remains of the dissected body.

And not just any body. People say it is Jonathan Wild's body.

CHAPTER 18

The End?

*T*he authorities could kill the man but they could not control the legend. To their astonishment, Jack became even more famous dead than he ever was alive.

Less than a fortnight after he was hanged, a pantomime called *The Harlequin Sheppard* was performed at the Drury Lane Theatre, in Jack's old neighbourhood.

Plays and pamphlets about Jack's life continued to appear for years after his death. Then in 1840 William Harrison Ainsworth wrote a novel called simply *Jack Sheppard*. It was an instant bestseller, and Jack's fame spread as far as Australia and America.

Once idolised by the poor apprentice boys of eighteenth-century London, Jack became a hero to the downtrodden factory boys of the nineteenth century. A hundred and twenty years after Jack's death at Tyburn, a government report into child labour noted that:

> *Some of the children have never heard of Her Majesty, nor such names as Wellington, Nelson, Buonaparte. But it is to be especially remarked, that among all those who had never heard such names as St Paul, Moses, Solomon, etc there was a general knowledge of the character and course of life of Dick Turpin, the highwayman, and more particularly of Jack Sheppard, the robber and prison-breaker.*

Glossary

Anatomisers Surgeons who dissected bodies in front of fee-paying spectators. They were allowed, by law, to dissect ten bodies a year of those hanged (grave-robbers and body-snatchers provided the rest).

Apprenticeship A system of contracting someone to a 'master' for seven years in order to learn a trade. Children as young as seven were apprenticed to chimney sweeps. Four out of every ten people hanged at Tyburn in the 18th Century were apprentices.

Baize A woollen cloth.

Ballad A popular song, often referring to real people and events of the day.

Beadle A parish official with the power to punish petty offenders.

Bedlam (Bethlehem Hospital) A grim mental hospital where visitors could come and laugh at the inmates, tipping the porter a penny as they left.

Cant A slang language of the London underworld.

Cesspits For collecting liquid waste from chamber pots etc.

Chamber pot A ceramic or pewter pot that served as a portable toilet. Men used them openly in front of each other and their contents were sometimes tipped out of open windows into the street outside.

Civil war Fighting between supporters of Parliament and supporters of the monarchy between 1642 and 1651. King Charles I was executed in January 1649. Oliver Cromwell ruled as Lord Protector between 1653 and his death in 1658, when the monarchy was restored under Charles II.

Coffee-house The first coffee-house in London opened in 1651, but there were soon hundreds of them. They were a place to read the papers or hold meetings, but they could be as rowdy as a tavern.

Coiner A maker of fake coins.

Cunning man A supposed wizard, consulted for medical remedies and to track down lost or stolen goods.

Debtor Someone who owes money.

Embezzlement Stealing money by fraud.

Entrails An animal's – or human's – insides or bowels.

Felon Someone guilty of a felony, a crime punishable by death.

Fetters Chains for the legs, to restrict movement.

Flash A showy, bragging way of talking. Flash ballads were sung about swaggering highwaymen going fearlessly to their deaths at the gallows – and about Jack of course.

Footpad A mugger.

Freak show An exhibition of abnormalities of nature, very popular in the 18th Century.

Frisk To search a person or their pockets.

Frost Fair Before its demolition in the 19th Century, the many arches of old London Bridge slowed down the flow of the Thames enough to allow it to freeze over in hard winters. During these 'frosts', fairs were held on the ice.

Fustian A coarse cotton fabric like corduroy.

Gallows A wooden frame for hanging those who were condemned to die. Tyburn was not the only one in London, and there would be a gallows in every town.

Great Fire Starting on September 2, 1666, in a baker's near London Bridge, it raged for four days, destroying thousands of houses, 87 churches, and old St Paul's Cathedral.

Hackney carriage A horse-drawn taxi. Modern London taxis are still called hackney carriages.

Hawker Someone selling their goods by shouting out in the street.

Hearse A carriage for carrying the dead.

Hemp A coarse fibre used to make rope like the one used by hangmen. Wives of those who were hanged were called hempen widows.

Halberd A long handled weapon, ending in a head that has both an axe and a point.

Harlequin A pantomime character who wears bright clothes and a mask and carries a magic wand.

Highwayman A robber, sometimes on horseback, who steals from people as they travel.

Huguenot A French Protestant.

Illiterate Unable to read.

Impeach To give evidence against someone, to 'peach' on someone.

Informer A person who gives information to the authorities. Thieves could get a royal pardon if their information led to the conviction of two other

thieves. Informers were described at the time as living 'by filthy means, like flies upon a turd'.

Jacobite A supporter of the exiled Stuart king James II and his descendants as claimants to the British throne.

Joiner A worker in wood, usually on small scale jobs.

Journeyman Someone whose apprenticeship is completed and can be hired by the day.

Leg irons Chains to restrict leg movement, such as fetters.

Lice The plural of louse. Lice are blood sucking parasitic insects that can carry typhus, a dangerous fever accompanied by red spots.

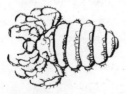

Lime kiln A furnace for making lime, for use in the building industry.

Maypole A tall pole decorated with greenery or flowers as part of a pre-Christian spring festival. On May 1 a folk dance was performed weaving ribbons around the pole. There were several maypoles in London and maypole dances were performed all over the country.

Moll One of many slang terms for a prostitute.

Night-soil man Someone who carried away the solid waste from chamber pots etc, from people's houses, sometimes selling it to farmers for fertiliser.

Noose A looped rope with a sliding knot used by the hangman. He would sell it by the inch after the hanging as souvenirs.

Old Bailey The location of the Sessions House since 1539, now the Central Criminal Court, which stands on the site of Newgate Prison following its demolition in 1902.

Pedlars Someone who 'peddles' or sells things in the street or door-to-door.

Periwig A large wig with a centre parting.

Piece-broker Someone dealing in fabrics that are of a standard length.

Pistol-whip To hit someone with a pistol.

Plague A deadly disease transmitted by rat fleas. The Great Plague of London of 1665 killed over 70,000 people.

Prosecute To bring before a court. Victims of crimes were responsible for prosecuting suspects.

Public executions Until the 19th Century, all executions in England were public and could attract huge crowds. After 1868 they were carried out in prisons until the death penalty was abolished in 1965.

Red kite A bird of prey that used to be common in towns as a scavenger.

Roundhouse A jail or lock-up.

Royal Society Formally constituted in 1660, it is the oldest scientific society in the world. Sir Christopher Wren was president from 1680-1, Sir Isaac Newton from 1703-26.

Running footman A uniformed servant who ran in front of his master's carriage or horse.

Sack A wine which was often served warm, as 'burnt sack'.

Service To be 'in service' meant to be a servant. Most servants were between 15 and 30 and often lived in their employer's house.

Sessions The times when the court is 'in session' or hearing cases.

Sexton A church officer who does various jobs like ringing the bell and digging graves.

Skittles A game (still played) in which the player tries to knock down wooden 'pins' with a ball.

Tavern A kind of pub.

Thief-taker The Blood Money Act of 1692 offered a reward of £40 for the catching, prosecution and conviction of highwaymen. Thief-taking became a profitable business.

Tumbril A two-wheeled, horse-drawn cart used for carrying dung – and those condemned to hang.

Turnkey A jailer.

Tyburn This was the main place of execution in London from 1388 to 1783. There is a stone marking the site of the gallows near present-day Marble Arch.

Vagabonds Homeless people.

Wise woman A woman supposedly skilled in magic, or astrology or medicine.

Index

Anatomisers *26, 79, 112, 118*

Bess, Edgworth *32, 34, 43-45, 49, 50-52, 59, 72*

Blake, Joseph (Blueskin) *53-58, 78-82, 98*

Constables *39, 45, 49*

Defoe, Daniel *93-94, 109-110, 112*

Field, William *56-59, 67-69, 79-80*

Geneva (Gin) *10, 32*

Hangings *11, 71, 77, 101-113, 116-118*

Highwaymen *26, 55, 70, 74*

Kneebone, William *19-27, 54-56, 67, 78*

London *7-18*

Newgate Prison *59-65, 69, 71-73, 75-78, 83-93, 95, 97-102, 115*

Old Bailey *41, 66-70, 72-74, 77, 95*

Page, William *73-75*

Prison
  Newgate Prison *59-65, 69, 71-73, 75-78, 83-93, 95, 97-102, 115*
  New Prison, Clerkenwell *49, 59*
  St Anne's Roundhouse *49-52*

St Clement's Roundhouse *38*
St Giles's Roundhouse *34, 45- 46*

Sheppard, Jack *32, 70*
  apprenticeship *28-29, 37-38*
  arrested *35, 37, 48, 59, 76, 91*
  birth *12-13*
  childhood *12-18, 19-22, 27-29*
  confessions *95-96*
  death *101-113*
  escapes *45- 47, 49-52, 71-76, 83-90*
  legend *119-120*
  thefts *34-35, 38, 43, 53-56*
  trials *66-70, 95*
Sheppard, Mary (mother) *13, 17, 37*
Sheppard, Thomas (father) *13, 17*
Sheppard, Tom (brother) *15, 43- 44*
Spitalfields *13, 15-16, 22, 36-37, 90*

Tyburn Gallows *11, 26, 71, 108, 120*

Wild, Jonathan *47, 67-68, 73-74, 78-80, 114-118*
  arrested *114*
  attacked *80-82*
  death *116-118*
  thief-taker *40-42, 58, 115*
  trial *115*
Wood, Owen *28-29, 32-38, 78*
Workhouses *17-18*